4 When the storm passes over land, the supply of moisture and heat is cut off, and the storm gradually slows down.

3 The entire storm starts to spin, and when it reaches 74 miles per hour, a Category 1 hurricane is born.

2 Winds begin to spiral upward and outward.

To my friend Jay Primiano, who taught me
the value of having access to the sea

ICANE

By John Rocco

L B

Little, Brown and Company
New York Boston

This is my dock.
Really, it's the neighborhood's dock,
but nobody ever comes here except me.
It's very old and splintery,
and it's my favorite place in the world.

It reaches way out over the river,
and from here I can fish or crab or swim
or just watch the minnows dart between the rocks.

One fine spring morning, after
Ojiisan had left to gather firewood,
his wife went to the stream to wash
clothes. While she was scrubbing and
rinsing, she looked up. There was a
huge ripe peach floating toward her.

"That looks delicious!" Obaasan
said to herself. "We'll have it for supper."

But the fruit bobbed far out in the
water. Stretch as she <u>might</u>, Obaasan
could not reach <u>it.</u> Then she recalled
an old charm verse. Clapping her hands
to the rocking of the peach, she sang:

> "Far water is bitter
>> Near water is sweet
> Leave the far water
>> And come to the sweet."

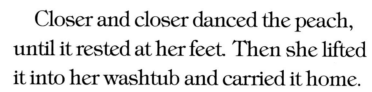

Closer and closer danced the peach, until it rested at her feet. Then she lifted it into her washtub and carried it home.

At sunset, when the woodcutter finally returned from the hills, Obaasan called, "I've been waiting for you all day. Look at the surprise I have!" And she showed him what she had found.

"What an enormous peach!" he said. "Where in the world did you get it?"

After she had told him the whole story, he said, "I'm glad you brought it home, because tonight I'm especially hungry. Hand me that big knife. I'll cut this peach in two, and we'll eat it right now."

But just as he brought the knife down on the fruit, a tiny voice shouted, "Wait a minute, Ojiisan!"

Suddenly the peach split wide open, and out stepped a baby boy.

"Heavens!" cried the two old people.

"Don't be frightened," said the baby. "I'm the answer to your prayers—the child of your old age."

Then the couple laughed with joy. "We will name you Momotaro, which means 'Peach Boy,'" they said, "because you were born from a peach."

Delighted by their good fortune, Ojiisan and Obaasan brought up the boy with love and tender care. Each bowl of rice, every dumpling they fed Momotaro made him grow bigger and stronger.

As the years passed, he became as brave as he was strong. Yet he was a friend to all the animals and a help to his parents.

When he was fifteen, Momotaro told Ojiisan and Obaasan, "I have grown up with the gifts of your kindness and wisdom. For these, I can never thank you enough. Now it is my turn to help others. I need to go to Onigashima, the *oni*'s island, and fight those terrible devils. For years, they have attacked and robbed our people. I want to punish the demons and bring peace to our land."

The old couple were afraid for their son to fight the wicked *oni,* but they were proud of his courage. Finally, Ojiisan said, "You have never been an ordinary child. Truly, you were sent to us as a gift from heaven. You may go with our blessing."

"We will make your favorite *kibi dango,*" added Obaasan. "Our dumplings will give you strength on your journey." After Ojiisan ground the millet seed, Obaasan cooked three *kibi dango* and wrapped them in a *furoshiki*, which she tied to Momotaro's belt. Then they gave him a sword, a war fan, and a banner of white silk embroidered with his emblem, the peach.

When it was time to part, the old couple had tears in their eyes. "*Sayonara!* Farewell! Come home to us safely," they called.

"*Sayonara,* dear parents," replied Momotaro. "Take care. I will return as soon as I can." Then he marched down the path alone.

Peach Boy walked and walked. When he got hungry, he sat down to eat one of his *kibi dango.* Just as he started to put it into his mouth, a big skinny dog came along.

"What have you there?" he asked, sniffing.

"One of the best *kibi dango* in all Japan," the boy answered. He saw that the animal was half-starved, and he thought, "I'm strong. I can do with one less dumpling." So he gave that *kibi dango* to the dog.

As soon as the dog had gobbled it down, he asked, "Who are you? Where are you going?"

"I'm Momotaro, the Peach Boy, and I'm going to Onigashima to fight the cruel *oni.*"

"I'll help you, kind Peach Boy," said the dog. And so the two of them went through the fields together.

As they entered the forest, a monkey swung down from a tree. He poked Momotaro's *furoshiki* and asked, "What have you there?"

"The best *kibi dango* in all Japan," Peach Boy answered.

"My, I'm hungry," said the monkey.

Momotaro thought, "I'm strong. I can do with two less dumplings." So he gave a *kibi dango* to the monkey.

After the monkey had nibbled it all, he asked, "Who are you? Where are you going?"

"I'm Momotaro, the Peach Boy, and I'm going to Onigashima to fight the wicked *oni*."

"I'll help you, brave Peach Boy," said the monkey. And so the three of them went through the forest together.

Before long, they heard a harsh cry overhead. A pheasant flew down to Momotaro, calling, "Help me! I can't find any food for my starving baby birds. What have you there in your *furoshiki*?"

"Just one *kibi dango,* the best in all Japan," Momotaro said. Then he thought, "I'm strong. I can do without any dumplings." So he gave the last *kibi dango* to the bird.

When the pheasant had shared it with his hungry chicks, he returned. "Who are you? Where are you going?" he asked.

"I'm Momotaro, the Peach Boy, and I'm going to Onigashima to fight the greedy *oni*."

"I'll help you, mighty Peach Boy," said the bird. And so the four of them went over the hills together.

At first the monkey and the dog quarreled, but Momotaro told them, "We will never defeat our enemy if we fight among ourselves." Then he ordered the monkey to march ahead carrying the banner, and the dog to march behind carrying the sword. Between the two marched Peach Boy, carrying his iron war fan. Under his command, the animals soon became faithful friends.

The troop traveled around the mountain and across a wide plain. The day had grown dark and cold when at last they reached the water's edge. A small boat was waiting for them on the shore. And there, far out in the fog, they could see the ugly *oni* castle.

Quickly the four boarded the sturdy little ship and headed toward Onigashima. An icy wind pushed them through the waves like an arrow. When they were near the island's rocky cliffs, Momotaro told the pheasant, "Go, warn the *oni* we are here."

Away he flew to the top of the castle wall and called down, "The great General Momotaro is coming to fight you! Surrender now! Break off your horns and give back the stolen treasure."

The *oni* roared, "HO, HO, HO! We're not afraid of a little bird, and we're not afraid of a Momotaro, either."

Meanwhile, Momotaro and the monkey and the dog had reached the castle gate. They set up a terrific racket: Momotaro shouted, the monkey shrieked, and the dog barked. The noise sounded like a great army. It made the king of the king of the *oni* bellow, "Who dares to knock at my gate?"

The young warrior called back, "It is Momotaro, the Peach Boy, and his soldiers. The best *kibi dango* in all Japan have given each of us the strength of a thousand!"

With that, the pheasant flew down and pecked the *oni*'s heads with his sharp pointed beak. He dodged their iron clubs and screeched and beat the air with his wings. It seemed to the *oni* that a thousand birds were attacking them.

At the same time, the monkey climbed over the wall and unlatched the gate. Rushing in with a battle cry, Momotaro began fighting the *oni* with his sword, while the dog growled and bit their legs, and the monkey screamed, pinched, and scratched them, and pulled their shaggy hair. The frightened enemy didn't know whether they were being fought by four or four thousand.

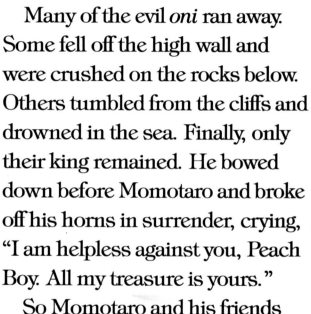

Many of the evil *oni* ran away. Some fell off the high wall and were crushed on the rocks below. Others tumbled from the cliffs and drowned in the sea. Finally, only their king remained. He bowed down before Momotaro and broke off his horns in surrender, crying, "I am helpless against you, Peach Boy. All my treasure is yours."

So Momotaro and his friends carried the *oni*'s treasure chest to their boat and sailed away, leaving the powerless king locked in his castle.

When the heroes returned, they gave the poor people the gold and silver that had been stolen from them. What was left they put on a cart, which Momotaro and the dog pulled and the monkey pushed, singing, *"Enyara, enyara, enyara ya"* all the way home. Ojiisan and Obaasan welcomed them with great happiness, and they all lived in peace and plenty for the rest of their lives.

SOURCE NOTES

 *"Mukashi, mukashi...*a long, long time ago," the traditional Japanese tale begins. Before writing was introduced to Japan, stories like *Momotaro* were told by village elders, wandering peddlers, and fortune-tellers. Traces of the prototype of *Momotaro* were recorded in A.D. 712. By the Edo period (1600–1868), this tale had become part of a genre of literature known as *kusazōshi*—fables, often including animals, that were performed by the puppet theater and by traveling professional storytellers. In the mid-1700s, some of these, including *Momotaro,* were transcribed and later published. Soon after the Meiji Restoration of 1868, when compulsory education for children was introduced, *Momotaro* was adapted for the government-compiled textbook used throughout Japan. In this way *Momotaro* passed from the oral tradition into a standard written version. Today it is said to be the most popular folktale of Japan, and it appears to have no analogue in folktales of other countries.

The character of Momotaro has long been held up to Japanese children as an example of kindness, courage, and strength. In ancient Japan, the *momo,* or peach, was believed to have a mysterious power for bringing happiness to people. *Taro* meant "first son" in old Japan, and

boys were named according to the order of their birth.

In the pictures of Momotaro on his quest, he is wearing an outfit resembling that of a warrior of the Kamakura period (1185–1336). His sword is fairly short and is worn blade downward, unlike those of the later *samurai.* The cloth tied around his head, as though to absorb sweat or blood, is symbolic of his will to work hard—in this case, to defeat the *oni.*

Momotaro is shown carrying a folding war fan, called a *gunsen.* The *gunsen* had nine ribs made of iron. Painted on one side of the heavy paper mount was a red sun on a gold background, and on the other a silver moon and stars on a black or dark blue background. Commanders on the battlefield used *gunsen* to signal to their soldiers.

The dog, or *inu,* appears frequently in Japanese folklore. As in our culture, he is thought of as a faithful protector. He is the traditional enemy of the monkey, however. When children quarrel, Japanese mothers sometimes say, "You are fighting like dogs and monkeys!"

There is only one species of monkey indigenous to Japan, a kind of short-tailed ape. According to Japanese folk wisdom, these *saru* can bring a family prosperity and ward off illness. *Saru* made of cloth, wood, or clay were often given to children as toys or attached to their clothing to drive away evil spirits.

The pheasant shown in this book is the *kiji (P. ver-*

sicolor), found only in Japan and now designated the national bird. The colorful male has always been admired for its beauty and has played a role in folklore since earliest times. *Kiji* have been known to perish shielding their chicks. It is said that when fire threatens the pheasants' eggs, the hen will lie on her back and hold them in her wings while the cock pulls her by her tail to safety.

Bloodcurdling stories are told of Japanese *oni,* demons who hurt, sometimes even devour, people. The demons have a frightening appearance. They wear only a tigerskin loincloth. Their form is basically human, but with knotty muscles, bulging eyes, fangs, claws, and red or blue skin. On their heads they sometimes have thick hair standing on end, and always one or two horns. Once these horns are broken off, however, *oni* become harmless.

The Japanese words used in this retelling are listed below. They should be pronounced with equal stress on every syllable. Singular and plural forms of nouns are indicated by context (e.g., one *oni* rules ten *oni*).

Enyara, enyara, enyara ya (en-yah-rah, en-yah-rah, en-yah-rah yah)—A work chant like the English "Yo ho heave ho."

Furoshiki (foo-roh-shee-kee)—A square of cloth used to wrap and carry things in.

Kibi dango (kib-bee dahn-go)—Dumplings made of pounded rice and millet dough.

Momotaro (Moh-moh-tar-oh)—The peach's first son.

Obaasan (oh-bah-sahn)—Honorable old woman or grandmother. A title of respect Japanese children might use for any elderly woman.

Ojiisan (oh-jee-sahn)—Honorable old man or grandfather. A respectful way to address any elderly man.

Oni (oh-nee)—Ogres or demons. Monsters who hurt human beings.

Onigashima (oh-nee-gah-shee-mah)—Island of the *oni. Shima* means "island" and *ga* is similar to "of."

Sayōnara (sigh-oh-nar-ah)—Goodbye, farewell.

For details of landscape, costume, and architecture, I consulted reproductions of Japanese narrative picture scrolls, *emaki,* from the twelfth through fourteenth centuries. During this period, Japanese handscroll painting experienced its greatest development and maturity. Illustrating folktales and supernatural religious sagas as well as scenes from daily life, these scrolls show the whole spectrum of medieval Japanese society, from the romance and intrigue of noblemen at court to the family life and work of commoners. The world of the *emaki* seemed to me to be the perfect fairytale setting for *Momotaro.*